DINK, JOSH, AND RUTH ROSE
AREN'T THE ONLY KID DETECTIVES!

WHAT ABOUT YOU?

CAN YOU FIND THE HIDDEN MESSAGE INSIDE THIS BOOK?

There are 26 illustrations in this book, not counting the one on the title page, the map at the beginning, and the picture of the cabin that repeats at the start of many of the chapters. In each of the 26 illustrations, there's a hidden letter. If you can find all the letters, you will spell out a secret message!

If you're stumped, the answer is on the bottom of page 137.

HAPPY DETECTING!

This one is for Parker Roy, man's best friend.
—R.R.

To all the national park rangers
—J.S.G.

Text copyright © 2019 by Ron Roy
Cover art copyright © 2019 by Stephen Gilpin
Interior illustrations copyright © 2019 by John Steven Gurney

Visit us on the Web!
SteppingStonesBooks.com
rhcbooks.com

Educators and librarians, for a variety of teaching tools,
visit us at RHTeachersLibrarians.com

Library of Congress Cataloging-in-Publication Data
Names: Roy, Ron, author. | Gurney, John Steven, illustrator.
Title: Grand Canyon grab / by Ron Roy ; illustrated by John Steven Gurney.
Description: New York : Random House, [2019] | Series: A to Z mysteries. Super edition ; 11 | "A Stepping Stone book." | Summary: The star of their favorite television show is kidnapped at the Grand Canyon, and it is up to Dink, Josh, and Ruth Rose to find him.
Identifiers: LCCN 2017048672 | ISBN 978-0-525-57886-4 (trade) | ISBN 978-0-525-57887-1 (lib. bdg.) | ISBN 978-0-525-57888-8 (ebook)
Subjects: CYAC: Kidnapping—Fiction. | Grand Canyon (Ariz.)—Fiction. | Mystery and detective stories.
Classification: LCC PZ7.R8139 Gp 2019 | DDC [Fic]—dc23

Printed in the United States of America
10 9 8 7 6 5 4 3 2

This book has been officially leveled by using the F&P Text Level Gradient™ Leveling System.

A to Z Mysteries®

SUPER EDITION 11

Grand Canyon Grab

by Ron Roy

illustrated by
John Steven Gurney

A STEPPING STONE BOOK™

Random House 🏠 New York

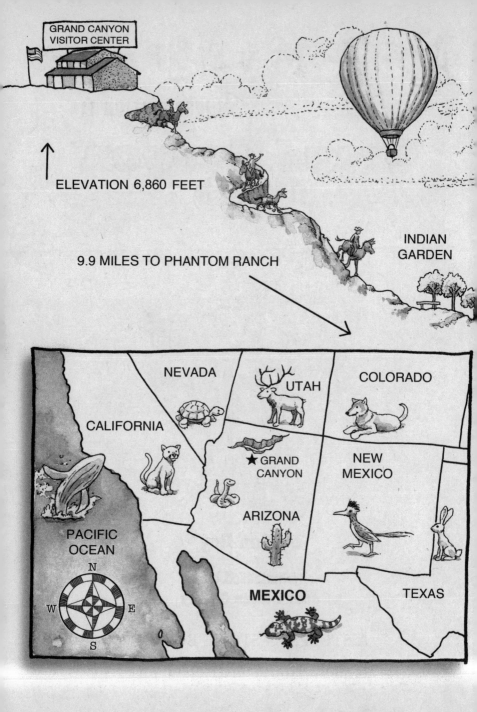

CHAPTER 1

"Josh, what are you doing?" Dink asked. He watched Josh slide five or six energy bars into his cargo pants pocket.

"I might get hungry," Josh answered.

"But we just ate breakfast!" Ruth Rose said, slipping her binoculars into her backpack. Ruth Rose liked her clothes to match. Today she was wearing red from her headband to her sneakers.

Josh grinned. "We did?" he asked. "Gee, I don't remember!"

"And we're having a picnic with my uncle in about two hours," Dink reminded his friend.

"Okay, *Donny*," Josh teased.

Dink's full name was Donald David Duncan, but most people called him by his nickname, Dink. His uncle had always called him Donny.

The kids were on their spring vacation in Arizona. Dink's uncle Warren Duncan had invited them to join him on a trip to the Grand Canyon. They were staying at Bright Angel Lodge. When Dink looked out his window, he could see the rim of the Grand Canyon.

Josh sat on his bed. "Actually, I'm a little nervous," he admitted. "And when I get nervous—"

"You eat!" Dink interrupted.

"Why are you nervous?" Ruth Rose asked.

Josh threw himself back on his pillow. "Well, let's see," he said, gazing up at the ceiling. "This morning, I go up a hundred miles in a hot-air balloon. Tomorrow I ride a donkey a hundred miles to the bottom of the Grand Canyon!"

Dink grinned. "It'll be a blast!" he said. "And it's not a hundred miles. The balloon only goes up about three miles, tops."

"Three miles!" Josh croaked. He closed his eyes and pretended to faint.

Ruth Rose opened her guidebook and read. "We'll be riding *mules* tomorrow, not *donkeys*," she said, pointing to a picture. "They look cute!"

Josh sighed. "Mules, donkeys, elephants . . . what's the difference?" He looked at Ruth Rose. "How far is it to the bottom?"

"Well, the canyon is a mile deep," she said, reading from her book. "But the ride is a little over nine miles, which will take about five hours."

"I have to sit on a mule for five hours?" Josh asked. "Do they bite?"

"Yeah," Dink said. "They bite nervous boys."

Ruth Rose checked the clock next to Dink's bed. "It's time for *Roger to the Rescue*," she said, turning on the TV. "That should relax you, Josh."

Josh sat up. "Cool! Roger's at the North Pole this week," he said.

Roger to the Rescue was their favorite TV show. It was about a kid named Roger Good and his pet parrot, Tommy. In each

show, Roger visited a different part of the world. He met people who were trying to help animals and the environment. The week before, Roger and Tommy had been in India, helping a scientist save a baby tiger trapped in quicksand.

"Scoot over!" Dink said. He and Ruth Rose jumped on Josh's bed as the show came on. First the kids saw a T-shirt with a circle on the front. Inside the circle were the letters *RTTR,* which stood for *Roger to the Rescue.*

The camera moved up to show Roger Good's face. He was played by Parker Stone, a teen actor. Roger put two fingers in his mouth and whistled. A gray parrot with a bright red tail flew to his shoulder.

In this episode, Roger and Tommy found two lost polar bear cubs and returned them to their mother. The final scene showed Roger sipping hot chocolate. Tommy was eating raisins out of a little purple box.

Then these words appeared on the TV screen: PLEASE VISIT ROGER AND TOMMY AT THEIR WEBSITE!

As the show ended, Josh let out a whistle.

"You sound just like Roger!" Ruth Rose said. She shut off the TV and grabbed her backpack. "Come on, we have to be in the lobby in two minutes!"

CHAPTER 2

The lobby of Bright Angel Lodge was busy and noisy. Guests were checking in and out. Hikers with backpacks stood around, drinking from water bottles and texting on cell phones.

Dink spotted his uncle talking to a tall man in shorts and a red shirt. The man's brown hair was tied in a ponytail. Uncle Warren waved, and the three kids hurried over.

"Kids, this is Randy Cane, your pilot," Uncle Warren said. "Ready to go up?"

"We're ready!" Dink told his uncle. The kids all shook hands with Randy.

"Does the balloon really go up a m-mile?" Josh asked.

Randy shook his head. "Not today," he said. "We'll only be up about three thousand feet."

"That's still pretty high, isn't it?" Josh asked.

"It's a little more than half a mile," Randy said. He smiled at Josh. "Are you afraid of heights, buddy?"

Josh gulped. "I'm just a little nervous," he admitted.

"Actually, I'm pretty nervous, too," Ruth Rose said. She nudged Dink and gave him a look.

"Yeah, I'm nervous, too!" Dink said, catching on. "I've never been in a hot-air balloon before."

Uncle Warren patted Josh's shoulder. "And I'm the most nervous because I'm the oldest!"

"I was plenty scared my first time, too," Randy said. "Let's get going, and I'll give you a balloon lesson while we drive."

They followed Randy outside, where it was sunny and mild. Dink stepped over a puddle near the lodge door.

"Thanks, you guys," Josh whispered.

"No problem," Dink said. "We can't let you be nervous all by yourself!"

Randy's van was sky blue. Both sides had been painted with pictures of hot-air balloons floating in the clouds.

Dink, Josh, and Ruth Rose slid into the seats behind Randy and Dink's uncle. They all clicked their seat belts. Randy drove out of the parking lot and headed away from the lodge.

"The balloon itself is just a giant bag," he began. "We call it the envelope, and it's made of real strong nylon. My balloon is shaped like an upside-down teardrop, with an opening at the bottom called the mouth. You'll be riding in a basket that hangs beneath the balloon."

"We're sitting in a basket half a mile

up in the sky?" Josh moaned.

"These are special baskets, my friend," Randy said. "They're made with super-strong steel. Very safe!"

"It must be a big basket, to fit all five of us," Uncle Warren commented.

Randy nodded. "Mine will hold us comfortably," he said. "But I've seen other baskets that carry eight people or more."

"How do you make the balloon go up?" Dink asked.

"We fill it with hot air," Randy said. "Since hot air is lighter than the air that surrounds the envelope, the balloon rises."

"Where do you get the hot air?" Josh asked.

"Great question," Randy said. "First I use a big fan to blow air into the envelope. Then I turn on my burner, which makes flames that heat the air. As the air gets warmer, the balloon floats up."

Randy pulled off the main road onto

a bumpy one. He steered his van across a broad field of grass and wildflowers. In the distance, the kids could see more hot-air balloons. Some were in the air with their baskets still on the ground. Other balloons were being filled with air by huge fans. The generators that operated the fans created a loud roar.

Randy parked next to a yellow balloon with blue stripes. Everyone climbed out of the van and stood near the balloon. The basket was on the ground, tied to wooden stakes. The envelope was already filled with air.

"This is mine," Randy said. He pulled a set of folding steps from inside the basket and set it on the ground. Then he helped Uncle Warren and the kids climb aboard. Uncle Warren snapped pictures of the other balloons.

They were standing in a square basket about ten feet on each side. The sides came up to Dink's chin, so nobody could fall out. Dink saw a coil of rope, a white food cooler, a toolbox, and a lumpy duffel bag. Tall metal tanks with PROPANE GAS stenciled on the surface stood against one side of the basket. Lying near the tanks was a rolled-up rug.

Randy's head appeared over the edge of the basket. "You folks all ready?" he asked.

"I guess so," Josh said.

Randy untied the cables from the stakes, quickly scrambled into the basket, and removed the steps. He yanked a valve on the burner, and flames shot up into the balloon's mouth.

"Hang on to the sides!" Randy shouted over the noise of the burner. "There are hats in that duffel if your ears get cold!"

The balloon began to float up. Dink looked over the side and watched the basket leave the ground. They rose higher and higher. Things below them grew smaller. Other balloons were in the sky around them. Some of the passengers waved to each other.

"This is so exciting!" Dink's uncle said. "I didn't think there would be so many other balloons!"

"There are thousands in the sky on a nice day," Randy said. "Three of my best friends own balloon companies."

"How are you feeling?" Dink asked Josh.

"I'm not sick yet!" Josh said.

Dink grinned. "Good. If you need to throw up, do it over the side!"

The three kids were thrilled to see birds flying past their balloon. Other balloons floated above and below them. Randy pulled on ropes that hung from the sides. "I'm opening vents to release a little hot air," he explained. "That lets me turn the balloon so you can see stuff all around us."

"Hey, there's the Grand Canyon!" Josh yelled.

"Yup. We're only a mile from the South Rim," Randy said.

The kids looked over the sides of the basket. Below them, the ground looked like a brown, green, and yellow patchwork quilt. Cars and trucks moved around like bugs.

It got cold, so Uncle Warren pulled ski hats from the duffel bag.

"See that red balloon?" Randy yelled, pointing over Dink's head. "That's my buddy Miguel. He has two passengers today. One of them is a kid a little older than you guys. When we stop for lunch, maybe you can say howdy."

"Where are we going for lunch?" Josh asked.

"I'm taking us to Blue Meadow for a

picnic," Randy said. "Real pretty place. Most of the balloon pilots stop there."

Ruth Rose trained her binoculars on the red balloon in the distance. At first, she saw only blue sky around it, but then she spotted the basket. She saw two men and a kid.

"Oh my gosh!" she yelled.

"What?" Dink asked.

"You're not going to believe who's in that basket!" Ruth Rose said.

"Who?" Josh asked.

Ruth Rose handed him the binoculars. "Who do *you* think it is?" she asked.

Josh peered through the glasses. "Jumping jackrabbits!" he said.

"Is it a rabbit?" Dink teased Josh.

Josh passed the binoculars to Dink. "Take a peek, Zeke," he said.

Dink looked, aiming the binoculars at the red balloon. "It's Roger Good!" he cried.

CHAPTER 3

"Who's Roger Good?" Randy asked the kids.

Dink handed the binoculars back to Ruth Rose. "He's the star of a TV show," he told Randy. "He has a parrot named Tommy. They rescue people and animals. It's a cool show!"

"I think it really *is* Parker!" Ruth Rose said, peering through the binoculars.

Uncle Warren laughed. "Now *I'm* confused. Who's Parker?" he asked.

"Parker Stone is the actor who plays Roger Good," Josh explained. "He knows a lot of awesome karate moves!"

"Lucky Miguel," Randy said. "He's got a TV star for a customer!"

The red balloon went higher, so Ruth Rose put away her binoculars.

Josh shared his energy bars. They all munched and enjoyed the sun, the sky, and the view.

"I'm taking us close to the edge of the Grand Canyon," Randy said, pointing.

The kids and Dink's uncle could see partway down into the canyon. The rock walls were red, yellow, and brown.

"I'm going down *there* tomorrow?" Josh gulped. "On a *mule*?"

"You'll have an awesome time," Randy said. "A lot of my customers like to hike or ride mules down there after their balloon ride. And a couple of miles from here, there's a spot where a truck or jeep can drive right to the banks of the Colorado River. Then you can get in a rubber raft and float down the river."

"That sounds really cool!" Dink said.

"Yeah, and there's a great place for staying overnight," Randy said. "It's called Phantom Ranch. You sleep in cabins built a hundred years ago."

"Phantom Ranch is where we're staying tomorrow night," Uncle Warren said. "I reserved two of those cabins."

"You'll love it," Randy said. "But watch out for scorpions and rattlesnakes!"

"Oh no!" Josh said.

"Just kidding, Josh. Those critters are afraid of humans," Randy said. "They run away when they hear you coming."

"I hope they run *fast*," Josh muttered.

Two hundred yards away, the red balloon was floating toward the ground.

"We're almost at Blue Meadow," Randy said. "When I tell you to, I want you to hold on and bend your knees. You'll feel a bump when the basket touches the ground."

He reached up and pulled on a metal ring. The kids heard a hissing noise above their heads.

"Now I'm letting out more hot air so we can float down," Randy explained. "We'll be on the ground in a few minutes!"

The kids looked over the side of the basket. They watched the land get closer and closer. Blue Meadow got its name from the millions of blue wildflowers that grew there. The meadow was at least a mile across, with a gravel road going through the middle.

The meadow stopped at the edge of the Grand Canyon. There was a fence so people wouldn't fall into the canyon.

"This is lovely," Uncle Warren said. "I can't wait to photograph all these wildflowers!"

"I'm going to try to land over by that stand of trees," Randy said. "I see my friend's balloon near that stream." He pointed to the red balloon, already on the ground.

The kids picked out Miguel's balloon from a lot of others in the meadow. Trucks, vans, and cars were parked along the stream. Blue Meadow looked like a busy place.

"Get ready!" Randy yelled. "Hold on and bend your knees!"

The kids grabbed the sides of the basket. Dink felt his ears pop.

They felt a bump, and some guys ran over and grabbed the basket. Randy threw ropes out, and the helpers tied the basket to some small trees. Then Randy placed the steps on the ground.

"Everyone okay?" Randy asked the kids.

"That was so amazing!" Josh said. "I'll never be nervous about floating in the sky again!"

"Nor will I!" Dink's uncle said. "You're an excellent pilot, Randy!"

Randy hopped over the edge of the basket onto the steps and helped Uncle Warren climb out. The kids clambered down and felt their feet touch the ground for the first time in an hour.

Randy's friend Miguel ran over. "What took you so long?" he teased Randy. "I've been down here ten minutes!"

Randy lifted the rug and picnic cooler from the basket. "Who's that in your party, Miguel?" he asked.

"The gentleman's name is Maxwell Kurve," Miguel said. "He's a TV agent or something. The kid is an actor on some TV show. His name is Parker Stone, and he has a parrot with him!"

"I was right!" Ruth Rose said.

Miguel walked back to his balloon. The kids and Dink's uncle unrolled the rug while Randy began taking food out of the cooler. Five minutes later, they were all sitting on the rug, eating sandwiches and cookies. They watched as the helpers let the air out of the yellow balloon. Randy poured them lemonade from a thermos. The grass around them was dotted with wildflowers. Butterflies floated among the blossoms.

A pickup truck with an orange rubber raft in the back roared past on the road. The tires blew dust into the air as the truck disappeared behind some trees.

"That guy must be going rafting on the river," Randy told the kids. "He can

drive his pickup down a trail straight to the water."

Miguel came over again to chat. He and Randy walked a few yards away, talking and laughing. Parker Stone and Maxwell Kurve were a hundred feet away, having lunch on their rug.

"Why don't you go say hi to Parker Stone?" Uncle Warren suggested.

"He's a big TV star," Josh said. "He'd never talk to us."

"Sure he would," Uncle Warren said. "I'm sure he'd love to know you're fans of his show."

"Okay," Ruth Rose said. "I want to get his autograph."

But before Ruth Rose could move, Parker and Maxwell Kurve began walking toward some trees. Tommy was perched on Parker's shoulder. They entered the woods and were out of sight.

"Too late, Ruth Rose," Josh said. "But you can have *my* autograph!" He whistled the way Roger did on the show. "I'm almost as good as Roger Good!"

Dink and Ruth Rose laughed.

A truck and van arrived and stopped near a balloon about ten yards away.

Some guys got out, unhooked the balloon from the basket, and loaded both into the back of the truck. They rolled up the nearby picnic rug and slid it in. The balloon passengers climbed into the van, and both vehicles pulled away.

Soon more trucks and vans arrived. Crews loaded the deflated balloons and their baskets.

Randy strolled over. "Time to pack up and head back to the lodge," he told the kids and Uncle Warren. "My partner will be here soon to load up our stuff. Fifteen minutes, okay?"

Just then, Maxwell Kurve ran out of the woods. His hair was mussed up, and his eyes looked wild. His nose, mouth, and chin were bright red, and his shirt was spattered with red stains.

He ran straight to Miguel, screaming, "Parker has been kidnapped!"

Dink realized the red stuff was blood.

CHAPTER 4

Dink, his uncle, Josh, Ruth Rose, and a few others ran over to Maxwell. Miguel handed him a towel to wipe his face and shirt, then pulled out his cell phone.

Randy helped Maxwell sit on the grass and gave him a bottle of water. "What happened, man?" he asked. "Where are you cut?"

"One of the kidnappers slugged me in the nose," Maxwell said, his voice shaky. "We were just walking and talking when they jumped us!"

His hands trembled as he tried to

wipe the blood from his face with the towel.

"Parker's producers are thinking about doing a show at the Grand Canyon," Maxwell went on. "We were talking about it, not really looking where we were going. Next thing, two guys wearing masks grabbed us! Parker started karate-kicking one of the guys, so they tied him to a tree. I tried to help him, and they tied me to another tree and threw a pillowcase over my head. I fought as hard as I could, and that's when one of them punched me in the face!"

Maxwell took some deep breaths. "I couldn't see anything through the pillowcase, but I heard them leaving, and then I managed to get untied. When I yanked the pillowcase off my head, Parker was gone!"

"I called the sheriff," Miguel said. "You want an ambulance?"

Maxwell shook his head. "I'm okay,"

he said, touching his nose. "It's stopped bleeding. I just can't believe this is happening!"

Randy looked across the meadow toward the trees. "You figure the kidnappers took the boy in a car or truck?" he asked.

Maxwell just shook his head again. "It all happened so fast I didn't see anything," he said.

"Where's Parker's parrot?" Dink asked.

Maxwell looked at Dink. "Tommy? I . . . I don't know," he said. "Maybe the kidnappers got him, too!"

Five minutes later, a truck roared up to the group. FLAGSTAFF SHERIFF was painted on one side. A man and woman wearing brown uniforms got out. Everyone watched the officers help Maxwell into their truck.

People started packing away their picnic things. More trucks and vans showed up. Balloons, baskets, and picnic stuff were loaded and driven away. The meadow was emptying.

Dink, Josh, and Ruth Rose kept an eye on the sheriff's truck. The two officers and Maxwell stepped out after several minutes. "Show us where it happened, sir," the female officer said. Maxwell led them toward the woods. Dink, Josh, and Ruth Rose followed while Randy and Uncle Warren cleaned up their picnic.

They went down a path next to the stream. It was cooler under the trees, and birds chattered over their heads.

Maxwell led the officers to a tree with yellow blossoms. Two empty plastic cups lay on the ground. "This is where they tied me," he said.

The male officer picked up a plain white pillowcase.

"They put that over my head," Maxwell said.

The officer examined the pillowcase, then slipped it inside a plastic bag.

The rope was still wrapped around the tree trunk. The female officer coiled it and slid it into another evidence pouch.

"Where was the boy?" she asked.

Maxwell pointed to a tree about fifty feet away. "I saw one guy drag him over there before the pillowcase went over my face," he said. "That's the tree they tied

Parker to when he tried to punch and kick the guy."

Dink spotted something pink under a bush. It was a mask like a pig's face. "I found something!" he called. The male officer ran over and picked up the mask.

"The one who grabbed Parker was wearing that!" Maxwell said. "The guy who tied me up wore a pirate face—you know, black eye patch and earring."

Maxwell pulled a cell phone out of his pocket. "I need to get back to the hotel," he said. "I have calls to make. This is . . . this is terrible!"

The officers gathered up the rope, pillowcase, plastic cups, and pig mask. They left the woods, talking quietly with Maxwell.

The kids stayed behind. They walked over to the tree where Parker had been tied. "He must've been scared," Ruth Rose said.

"I wonder where Tommy is," Josh said.

Dink was looking at the ground near the tree. "Guys, check this out," he said, pointing to some scrapes in the dirt. "What do you suppose those are?"

Josh knelt down and peered at the spot. "Some kind of weird marks," he said. "Maybe it's a code!"

Ruth Rose stood next to Dink and looked at the marks. She turned around with her back to the tree, then looked at them again. "They're letters," she said. "You were looking at them upside down."

Dink and Josh moved to stand beside Ruth Rose. "You're right!" Dink said. "They *are* letters: *T, O, M, R, A, N.*"

"Is that a word?" Josh asked.

"I think it's two words," Ruth Rose said. "There's a space between *TOM* and *RAN.*"

The three kids stared at the letters in the dirt.

"Parker was tied to this tree," Josh said. "So maybe he wrote the letters!"

"If he was tied, how *could* he write anything?" Ruth Rose asked.

"Easy peasy," Josh said. He leaned his back against the tree trunk. "Okay, I'm tied up. I can't use my hands. But I can move my feet!"

Pointing the toe of his sneaker, Josh

drew the letters *T, O, M* in the dirt.

"Parker wrote it with his foot!" Ruth Rose cried. "You're a genius!"

"I know, Moe," Josh said.

"But who's *Tom*?" Dink asked.

"Maybe one of the kidnappers?" Josh said. "What if this *Tom* dropped his mask and Parker saw his face and recognized him!"

"Okay, but why would Parker write *TOM RAN*?" Dink asked. "*Why* did Tom run? *Where* did he run?"

"Could *TOM* be short for *Tommy*?" Ruth Rose asked. "Maybe Parker was trying to tell Tommy to run away from the kidnappers!"

"That definitely says *RAN*," Josh said. "That's an *A*, not a *U*. Besides, wouldn't Parker tell his parrot to *fly* away, not *run* away?"

"So where *is* Tommy?" Dink asked. He looked up into the tree. The leaves were thick, so he couldn't see much up there. "Josh, do Roger Good's whistle."

Josh put two fingers in his mouth and whistled. The kids stared up into the branches. "Do it again," Dink said.

Josh repeated the sound. Suddenly they heard a squawk. Something gray burst out of the leaves and landed on Josh's shoulder. *"Rescue Roger!"*

It was Tommy!

CHAPTER 5

"Good parrot!" Josh said. He stroked the bird's feathers.

"Tommy looks really upset," Ruth Rose said. "He must have seen the kidnappers grab Parker."

The parrot flapped his wings and squawked, "Rescue Roger!"

"Tommy, who *took* Roger?" Dink asked.

Tommy didn't say anything. He ruffled his feathers and made small clicking noises.

The kids headed back toward Blue Meadow with Tommy. They walked along the narrow stream, watching the water tumble over rocks.

"Wait a sec, guys," Ruth Rose said. "I see litter." She grabbed a white plastic bag that was caught on a tree branch. Then she picked up a paper plate and a plastic fork and dropped both into the bag.

Dink spotted a soda can and a piece of a foam cup and added them to the bag. Josh picked up a plastic sandwich container and a hunk of aluminum foil.

As they stepped out from under the trees, Ruth Rose found a small bottle at the edge of the stream. It was heart-shaped and had a twist cap. The little container was half-filled with red liquid, and the label said REALLY RED!

"It's nail polish," Ruth Rose said. "What a pretty bottle!" She slipped it into her pocket as they walked back to Blue Meadow.

Randy and Uncle Warren were waiting for them.

"Hey, you found the kid's parrot!"
Randy said.

"He was up in the tree where the kidnappers tied Parker," Josh said. "I'll bet
he saw everything!"

"Does he talk?" Uncle Warren asked.

"Tommy, who took your friend away?"
Dink asked. "Who took Roger?"

Tommy flapped his wings and said,
"Rescue Roger!"

"Miguel is really bummed out," Randy
said. "I've never seen him so upset."

Dink looked around. He didn't see the
red hot-air balloon. "Did Miguel leave?"
he asked.

Randy nodded. "Yup. He followed the
officers into town," he said. "They wanted
to question him after they dropped off
Mr. Kurve at his hotel."

The kids and Dink's uncle climbed
into the van, and Randy drove across the
meadow, following tire marks from the
other vehicles. Josh held Tommy on his

lap, smoothing his feathers.

They told Randy and Uncle Warren how the officers had found the white pillowcase the kidnappers put over Maxwell's head.

"One of the kidnappers dropped his mask," Ruth Rose said. "It was a pig's face."

"And we think Parker wrote a message in the dirt," Josh added. He described the six letters they'd seen.

"Maybe someone else wrote that yesterday or last week," Randy suggested. "A lot of people picnic by the stream under those trees."

Dink thought about the puddle he'd almost stepped in, back at the lodge. "It rained last night," he said. "If those letters had been there before today, wouldn't they have washed away?"

Randy nodded. "You're right. It did rain last night." He grinned. "That's why my van looks so clean!"

"My nephew has an excellent memory!" Uncle Warren said.

When they reached Bright Angel Lodge, they thanked Randy for a great adventure.

"So you're going down into the canyon on mules tomorrow?" he asked.

Dink's uncle nodded. "Yes. Where I live, in New York City, I ride in taxis and subway trains," he said. "I must take pictures so my friends can see me on a mule!"

"That's awesome," Randy said. "Wish I was going, but some schoolteachers have booked my balloon for the morning."

Randy pulled away, and the kids followed Uncle Warren into the lobby. No one seemed to care that Josh had a parrot on his shoulder. In the elevator, Tommy nibbled on Josh's ear.

"Stop that!" Josh said.

"Stop that!" Tommy repeated, sounding just like Josh.

"I'm going to read and have a nap," Uncle Warren said when they reached his room. "How about pizza later on?"

"How about right now?" Josh said.

Uncle Warren laughed and stepped into his room. "Donny, will you order pizza for five o'clock?"

"Okay, Uncle Warren," Dink said. He unlocked his and Josh's room door, and the kids went in and dumped their stuff.

"I still can't believe Parker Stone got kidnapped," Ruth Rose said. "And we were there!"

Dink opened the mini fridge and took out three bottles of water. "I'll bet the kidnapping was planned ahead of time," he said.

Dink handed Josh and Ruth Rose each a water. "Those guys must've been *waiting* for Parker in the woods."

Josh poured some of his water into a cup for Tommy. "But how did the kidnappers know he was riding in a hot-air balloon today?" he asked.

"Right, and how did they know he'd go for a walk in *those* woods?" Ruth Rose added. "There were a lot of other places to walk."

"Somebody must have tipped them off," Dink said. "Somebody who *knew* that Mr. Kurve and Parker would be in Blue Meadow today."

"Like who?" Josh asked. Then he said,

"Randy knew! Maybe *RAN* was short for *Randy*!"

Dink shook his head. "Randy had never heard of Parker Stone before this morning," he said.

"How about Miguel?" Josh asked. "*He* must have known, because he was their pilot!"

Dink and Ruth Rose stared at him.

"Guys, it makes sense," Josh went on. "Mr. Kurve calls Miguel and orders the balloon, probably weeks ago. He tells Miguel about Parker's TV show. Miguel figures Parker is worth a lot of money, so he hires those two guys to grab him!"

"I don't know," Dink said. "Maybe Miguel *did* find out Parker was famous, but that doesn't mean he kidnapped him."

"And we saw how upset Miguel was when Mr. Kurve told us what happened," Ruth Rose added.

"Okay, so not Randy and not Miguel," Josh said. "Who else knew that Parker

Stone was going on a hot-air balloon ride?"

No one had an answer.

Tommy walked around the room, exploring everything he saw. His toenails made clicking noises on the wood floor.

Josh sprawled out on his bed. "Is it pizza time yet?" he asked.

CHAPTER 6

Dink called the lobby.

"Hi, this is Taylor at the front desk," a man said. "How can I help you, Mr. Duncan?"

Dink smiled at being called *Mr. Duncan*. He asked Taylor how to order pizzas.

Taylor said he would do it, and Dink asked for two large pizzas with everything.

Tommy flew up onto the bed and landed on Josh's stomach. "Tommy loves pizza!" the bird said.

"Oh my gosh, I just thought of something!" Josh said. "What do we do with

Tommy when we go down into the canyon tomorrow?"

"Maybe we can bring him with us," Ruth Rose said.

"On a mule?" Josh said.

"Let's go ask Taylor," Dink said.

The kids went to the lobby. Tommy rode on Josh's shoulder, nibbling on his hair.

"Cut it out," Josh said. "I don't need a haircut!"

"Haircut!" Tommy said.

They walked up to the desk.

Taylor smiled at the kids. "Hi there," he said. "Rooms twelve, thirteen, and fourteen, right? Two large pizzas?"

"Right," Dink said. "I'm Dink, and this is Ruth Rose. The guy with the parrot is Josh."

"Cool!" Taylor said. "Does he talk?"

"Josh talks a lot!" Dink said. Then he laughed. "The parrot does, too." He told Taylor they were all going into the canyon tomorrow on mules. "But we don't know what to do with Tommy."

"We're staying down there overnight," Ruth Rose said.

"Can we bring him with us?" Josh asked.

Taylor tapped his fingers on the counter. "It's possible," he said. "A few weeks ago, a woman took her cat down with her. Fluffy rode in a special carrier tied to the mule's saddle."

"Great!" Josh said. "Where can I get a carrier?"

"First you have to ask the ranger in charge of the mule rides," Taylor said. "I'll try to find a cat carrier for you."

"Awesome!" Josh said. "Where's the mule guy?"

"It's a mule *gal*," Taylor said. "Actually, she's my girlfriend." He pointed through the lobby door. "Go out, take a right, and walk over to the barn. Ask for Lisa."

The kids followed Taylor's directions.

They found the mule barn on the other side of the parking lot. A bunch of brownish-gray mules stood inside a corral. A woman with curly hair was filling a water trough with a hose.

Dink walked up to the corral. "Hi," he said. "Are you Lisa?"

The woman smiled. "I sure am," she said. "And I'll bet you're the kids going on a mule ride tomorrow!"

"We can't wait!" Dink said. "My uncle is coming, too. He said we're sleeping in a cabin at Phantom Ranch!"

"Your uncle must be pretty special," Lisa said. She reached a finger toward Tommy. "What's his name?"

"Tommy," Josh said. He told Lisa they didn't know what to do with Tommy when they went to the bottom of the canyon. "Taylor told us you let a woman take her cat down with her."

"Taylor's right, but we don't usually let pets go into the canyon," Lisa said, stroking Tommy's wing feathers. "That woman's cat needed medicine every day, so we made an exception for her."

"How about Tommy?" Josh asked. "He's already upset because his owner got kidnapped and—"

"Whoa," Lisa interrupted him. "Who

got kidnapped?" The kids explained what had happened at Blue Meadow.

"You're kidding me, right?" Lisa said. "My little sister loves Roger Good! She never misses *Roger to the Rescue*! The actor got kidnapped? Why didn't I see it on the news?"

"It just happened," Dink told her. "Some officers came. I guess they're investigating."

"We found his parrot in a tree, and I'm taking care of him for a while," Josh said.

"I know the two wranglers who will be your guides tomorrow," Lisa said. "I'll tell them about the parrot. But don't let Tommy out of your sight. There are coyotes and mountain lions in the canyon who would love to eat a parrot for lunch!"

"I'll watch him, don't worry!" Josh said.

"Can we pet the mules?" Ruth Rose asked.

"Sure, and by the end of your trip

down, they'll be your best friends!" Lisa said. "Be here by seven tomorrow morning, okay?"

The kids spent some time petting the mules. Tommy stood tall on Josh's shoulder, watching the big animals inside the corral. He flapped his wings and clicked his beak.

"Their ears are so soft!" Ruth Rose said.

"Soft!" Tommy said.

An hour later, the kids were in Dink and Josh's room, eating pizza at the table. Dink's uncle was snapping pictures of Tommy. The parrot was on the floor, pecking at a piece of crust.

"I wonder where Parker Stone is right now," Josh said quietly.

Uncle Warren looked at his watch. "Maybe it's on the news," he said. He got up and turned on the TV.

At first, there was weather, then sports, then a shampoo commercial.

A man's face appeared. He looked worried as he read from his notes:

A fourteen-year-old boy was kid-napped today near the Grand Canyon. Parker Stone, the star of the TV series Roger to the Rescue, *was with his agent, Maxwell Kurve.*

Mr. Kurve told our reporter they were having a picnic lunch at Blue Meadow when two masked men abducted Parker Stone.

"The men were hiding in some trees. They surprised us and grabbed Parker," Mr. Kurve said. "The kidnappers put a pillowcase over my head and tied me to a tree. When I fought back, one of the masked men struck me in the face."

Nothing has been heard from the boy's abductors. Police are asking anyone who might have information to call the Flagstaff Sheriff's Office.

Dink's uncle shook his head and turned off the TV. He began clearing the table. "Do you think the kidnappers knew Parker was going to be in that spot today?" he asked.

"We wondered the same thing!" Ruth Rose said.

"I think they knew, and I think they were waiting there for him," Dink told his uncle. "They had the pillowcase, ropes, and masks with them!"

Everyone thought about that for a minute.

"I wonder how they got Parker out of Blue Meadow," Josh said.

They all looked at him.

"I mean, where did the kidnappers go after they grabbed him?" Josh asked.

"We saw a lot of cars and trucks there," Ruth Rose said. "Maybe they put Parker in one and just drove away."

"But wouldn't someone notice two guys shoving Parker into a car?" Josh asked.

Uncle Warren shrugged. "Well, they did it somehow, and quickly," he said. "Donny is right—the kidnapping must have been planned ahead of time."

They finished cleaning up. Ruth Rose and Uncle Warren went to their rooms, across the hall from the room Dink and Josh shared.

Dink brushed his teeth, put on his pajamas, and climbed into bed. In the other bed, Josh was already snoring.

Tommy was perched on Josh's headboard with his beak tucked under one wing.

Dink shut off the light and tried to get comfortable. He was almost asleep when his eyes popped open. A thought buzzed in his brain like a fly in a bottle. What was it? Something he had seen or heard when they were with the officers in the woods. He remembered the white pillowcase, the plastic cups, the rope, the pig mask. The officers had taken them all away.

Drifting toward sleep, Dink could still see the scene Maxwell Kurve had described. Two masked men had grabbed him and tied him to a tree. A pillowcase was pulled over his head. Someone punched him in the nose, making him bleed.

If that was how it happened, Dink wondered, why wasn't there any blood on the pillowcase?

CHAPTER 7

Early the next morning, the kids and Uncle Warren walked to the mule corral. Near the barn, six saddled mules were waiting, their long ears swishing at flies. Saddlebags carrying water and other supplies hung down their flanks. The mules watched the kids approach with curious brown eyes.

"Good morning!" Lisa called through the barn's wide door. "Be right with you!"

Uncle Warren and the kids wore pants and long-sleeved shirts. They had smeared sunblock on their faces and hands. Fanny packs were tied around their waists, and they each carried a backpack.

Tommy was inside a cat carrier. "Stay cool," Josh told the parrot. "There's no need to be nervous!"

Dink laughed. "Tommy is fine," he said. "It's you I'm worried about!"

Ruth Rose petted one of the mules on the nose. "I wonder which is mine," she said. Her shirt, headband, and pants were yellow today. Even her sneakers and backpack were the color of daffodils.

Lisa and two men walked out of the

barn. One of the men was tall and had gray hair. His partner was shorter and younger. They both wore cowboy hats, jeans, and flannel shirts.

"That's Poppy, and she can be your mule for today if you like," Lisa told Ruth Rose. "She's very sweet."

Lisa walked up to Uncle Warren. "You must be the nice uncle the kids told me about," she said, holding out her hand. "Lisa Bloom."

"Warren Duncan," Uncle Warren said, shaking hands with Lisa.

Lisa introduced the two wranglers. "The tall guy is Luke," Lisa said. "His sidekick there is Junior. These fellas know the canyon, the trail, and every mule in the barn. You're in good hands!"

"Smile, everyone!" Uncle Warren called out. He took pictures of Luke, Junior, and Lisa standing next to Dink, Josh, and Ruth Rose. Then he asked Junior which was his own mule.

"You'll be on Oliver," Junior said. "He's a sweetheart."

Uncle Warren handed Junior his camera, stuck his foot in a stirrup, and pulled himself onto Oliver's saddle. Uncle Warren smiled, and Junior snapped his picture.

"You kids ready?" Luke asked.

"I've been ready since last week!" Ruth Rose said.

Luke cupped his hands to make a step for Ruth Rose's left foot, and boosted her onto Poppy's saddle. "Just hold the reins loosely," he told her.

"My feet can't reach the stirrups," Ruth Rose said.

Luke adjusted the left stirrup and slipped her yellow sneaker into it. Then he did the same with the right stirrup. "Comfortable?" he asked.

"Thank you," Ruth Rose said. "Poppy thanks you, too!"

Josh's mule was Sleepy, and Dink's

mule was named Rambler. Luke's mule was Joe, and Junior rode one called Flo.

When everyone was saddled up, Lisa tied Tommy's carrier securely on the back of Sleepy's saddle, behind Josh. She tucked a towel around the carrier to keep out the sun.

"It's dark in here!" Tommy called out, making everyone laugh.

"We ride single file, and I'll be in front," Luke informed the group. "Ruth Rose will ride behind me, then Josh, then Dink, followed by his uncle. Junior will take up the rear."

"I always get the rear," Junior said with a big grin. "These mules know exactly what to do, folks. You don't have to steer them or anything. Just let them follow the mule in front of them."

Lisa arranged the mules into a line behind Luke. "Have fun, everyone!" she said. "I'll see you tomorrow!"

"If anyone has a problem, just give out

a yell," Luke told the group. "We'll stop halfway down for lunch and a chance to stretch your legs."

"Can I use my cell phone down in the canyon?" Dink's uncle asked.

Luke shook his head. "There's no reception," he said. "But there's a landline in the park ranger's hut."

"Okay, thanks," Uncle Warren said. "So should I shut my phone off now?"

"Good idea," Luke said. "These mules aren't used to hearing ringtones, and the sound might scare them."

"Right. Let me check something first." Uncle Warren tapped a news app on his phone, read something, then powered off.

He leaned forward over Oliver's neck and whispered, "Donny, Parker Stone's parents received a ransom note."

Dink turned in his saddle and stared at his uncle.

Uncle Warren held up three fingers. "Three million dollars!" he said.

CHAPTER 8

Dink gulped. He wanted to enjoy the mule ride, but he couldn't stop thinking about Parker Stone. Who took him? How did they spirit Parker away from Blue Meadow without anyone noticing? Where was Parker now?

Luke whistled and said, "Git along, Joe," to his mule.

Joe moved forward, and the other mules followed. Dink saw a sign that said BRIGHT ANGEL TRAIL next to a rocky path that led down into the Grand Canyon.

The trail was about four feet wide. The right side was a steep rock wall. On

the left were only space and the canyon floor, miles below them. The mules
placed their hooves carefully as they
moved downward.

"Everybody doing okay?" Luke called
over his shoulder.

"Yes!" Ruth Rose shouted. So did Josh,
Dink, Uncle Warren, and Junior.

"Okay, enjoy the ride and this beau-
tiful morning!" Luke said. "Should take
us about five hours. If you look across
the canyon, you'll see the North Rim.
It's about ten miles from the South Rim,
where we are."

"And check out the rock formations,"
Junior called out. "You're looking at the
inside of the earth!"

The mules trotted down the trail, past
layers of colored rock in the canyon wall.
Far below, Dink could see the twinkle of
the sun on the Colorado River.

Small plants grew on the edge of the
trail, and lizards darted away from the

mules' hooves. A bird flew in front of Rambler, and the mule brayed loudly.

Dink felt safe sitting on Rambler's back. He leaned forward and called out to Josh, "How are you and Sleepy doing?"

Josh turned and grinned. "Piece of cake," he said. "At least today I'm only a few feet off the ground!"

From the end of the line, Junior began to sing a funny song about a cowboy writing a love letter to his girlfriend. Everyone laughed.

The mule train went down and down and down. Dink sipped from his water bottle and enjoyed feeling the sun on his shoulders. He talked to Rambler, saying, "Good mule, good mule!" Rambler swished his ears and nodded.

The group stopped twice at rest areas along the trail. Dink was glad he'd worn long sleeves. He finished his bottle of water, wishing he had more.

"Next stop is Indian Garden for

lunch!" Luke informed them. "Hope you're hungry!"

"I am!" Josh called from atop Sleepy.

Indian Garden was a small campground shaded by trees. Junior showed them a water spigot, where they refilled their bottles. Picnic tables and benches stood under the trees.

Luke led the group to a shady spot. "Let's eat!" he said. He unbuckled Joe's saddlebags and carried plastic bags to one of the picnic tables.

Everyone climbed off the mules and headed for the food. Dink's legs felt wobbly, and his bottom was sore. Junior gave the mules some water and let them munch on grass.

Josh peeked in the cat carrier to check on Tommy. The parrot's head was tucked under a wing, so Josh let him sleep. He set the carrier beneath a bench, out of the sun.

Luke placed six white boxes on the

table. Three were marked with the letter *T* and three with *P*.

"What do the letters stand for?" Josh asked.

"Sandwich choices," Junior said. "*T* stands for *tarantula and tomato,* and the *P* is for *porcupine with pickles.*"

"I'm not eating any spider!" Josh yelped.

"Don't listen to Junior," Luke said. "The *T* is for *tuna,* and *P* is for *peanut butter.* They're both great!"

Dink and his uncle each chose tuna. Josh and Ruth Rose took peanut butter. Luke and Junior flipped a coin. Junior won and took the other tuna box.

Each box held a sandwich, a bottle of water, an apple, and a chocolate brownie.

"I'm going to get a few pictures of this magnificent place!" Dink's uncle said. He picked up his sandwich and wandered off with his camera.

While Dink ate, he looked up at the

canyon wall. The rock was in layers of different colors: orange, red, yellow, brown. He smiled, remembering a cake his grandmother had made for a birthday. The cake was layered with yellow custard, dark chocolate, and red raspberry. The red made Dink recall the blood on Maxwell Kurve's face and shirt.

But then he remembered what had bothered him last night. He whispered to Josh and Ruth Rose, "Guys, don't you wonder why there wasn't any blood on that pillowcase?"

"What pillowcase?" Josh asked around a mouthful of sandwich.

"The one the kidnappers put over Mr. Kurve's head when they grabbed Parker," Dink said. "They punched him and he had a bloody nose, so why wasn't there any blood on the pillowcase?"

Ruth Rose put her sandwich down. "You're right," she said. "The pillowcase was clean when that officer found it. It looked brand-new!"

"So Mr. Kurve must have gotten it wrong," Josh said. "Maybe he got his bloody nose *before* they put the pillowcase over his face. The guy was pretty freaked out, remember."

Dink watched his uncle snapping pictures of the mules where they munched grass. "Maybe," he said.

Ruth Rose read to them from her guidebook, "Scientists think the Grand Canyon was formed millions of years ago as the Colorado River slowly eroded its way down through miles of rock."

"And the river is still flowing," Luke said. "So the canyon is getting a tiny bit deeper every day!"

The kids placed their trash and water bottles in their backpacks. Ten minutes later, they were all mounted and in line behind Luke. The mules headed farther down the Bright Angel Trail. Dink felt himself closing his eyes. The rocking of Rambler's gait, the creak of the saddle, and the warm breeze on his face nearly put him to sleep.

The trail leveled off, and they were on the canyon floor. Luke led them across a wood bridge that took them to the north side of the Colorado River. The mules' hooves clip-clopped on the boards.

Dink looked down into the river. The

greenish-brown water tumbled along beneath the bridge. It was hard to believe that this river had been flowing for millions of years.

On the other side of the bridge, the mules started walking faster. They tossed their heads and hee-hawed loudly.

"The mules know we're almost there!" Luke called over his shoulder. "They can smell the hay in the barn. Phantom Ranch is on the other side of that stand of trees."

CHAPTER 9

Five minutes later, they were on a dirt road. The mules trotted beneath a sign that hung over the path. As they passed under it, Dink read PHANTOM RANCH.

Luke slowed Joe in front of two cabins standing under shade trees. The cabins looked old. They were built of river stones and thick wood beams. Sunlight glinted off the windows.

Across a creek were two more cabins. All the cabins had stone chimneys, and the roofs were painted dark green.

"Here's where you'll bunk down tonight," Luke told them. "Cabin number

74

two has bunk beds for the kids. Mr. Duncan, you'll be next door in number one. Both cabins have a sink, toilet, and kitchen. There's a shower building over by the mule barn. You can get snacks from the canteen, but meals are served in the dining lodge on the other side of those trees."

The kids and Uncle Warren dismounted. Their hands and faces were sweaty and covered with trail dust. They all thanked Luke and Junior.

While his uncle snapped pictures of their cabins, Dink quietly told Josh and Ruth Rose about the ransom for Parker Stone. The two just stared at him with wide eyes.

"How do you all feel?" Luke asked the kids.

"My bottom is sore, and my mouth could use some ice cream!" Josh said.

Luke laughed. "I'm sure you can get ice cream at dinner tonight," he said.

"Your rear will feel better tomorrow."

Josh untied the cat carrier and set it on the ground. Tommy flapped his wings and let out a squawk.

"See y'all later!" Junior said as he and Luke led the mules to the creek for a drink.

"I need a nice, long shower," Dink's uncle said. "What are you kids going to do?"

"I think we'll go exploring," Dink said.

"Good idea," Uncle Warren said. "I've read there may be gold deposits around here. Maybe you'll find some!"

"Awesome!" Josh said.

Uncle Warren opened his cabin door and stepped inside.

The kids walked up their cabin's steps. The door creaked when Dink opened it. Inside, it was dark and smelled old.

Dink put his hand on Josh's arm.

"Shhh," he said. "I heard something moving in there!"

Ruth Rose poked Josh. "No problem, it's just a rattlesnake," she said.

"No," Dink said. "A whole *family* of rattlesnakes!"

"Ha ha," Josh said. "You need better jokes, folks!"

The kids stepped inside the cabin, and Dink flipped a light switch on the wall. "Wow, this is so cool!" he said.

They were in a simple living room. A table and chairs stood on a red-and-blue rug in front of the fireplace. A box of postcards and a pen lay on the table. Books and board games filled a bookshelf.

A small fridge, stove, and sink were built against one wall. Opposite them was a door to a bathroom. Dink pushed open another door, which led into a bedroom.

There were two sets of bunk beds. Each bed was covered with a red blanket, and there were ladders for climbing to the top bunks.

Josh set the cat carrier on the floor. "Do you want top or bottom bunk?" he asked Dink.

"Top," Dink said. He took off his backpack and threw it onto his bunk.

"So I get two beds!" Ruth Rose said. She plopped her pack onto the lower bed of the other bunk.

Josh let Tommy out of the cat carrier. The parrot ruffled his feathers, flew up to the ceiling, and landed on a beam.

Josh looked up. "Are you going to sleep there?" he asked.

"Sleepy Tommy!" Tommy said. He tucked his head under a wing.

"I guess he'll be all right," Dink said. "He'll come down when he's hungry."

"Speaking of being hungry," Josh said, "I don't have any food for Tommy."

"He eats raisins on TV," Dink said.

"In the jungle, parrots eat fruit," Ruth

Rose said. "Maybe we can get something for Tommy tonight at supper."

Ruth Rose pulled her flashlight, Swiss Army knife, and binoculars from her fanny pack. She found the half-empty nail polish bottle. "How would I look with red nail polish?" she asked.

"I don't think red goes with yellow," Josh said, shaking his head.

Ruth Rose sat on her bed and twisted the top off the bottle. "That's funny," she said, sniffing the bottle. "This doesn't smell like nail polish."

"What does it smell like?" Dink asked.

"Kind of sweet, like cupcakes," Ruth Rose said.

"Stop teasing!" Josh said.

Ruth Rose closed the bottle and set it on a little shelf next to her bed.

Dink started to leave the bedroom. "Let's go check out this place," he said.

"Maybe we'll see the phantom!" Ruth Rose said, following Dink.

"What phantom?" Josh asked, looking worried.

Ruth Rose smiled. "How do you think Phantom Ranch got its name?" she asked. "My guidebook says the phantom is invisible. He sneaks around at night, looking for boys with red hair!"

Josh burst out laughing. "You're scary, Mary!"

The kids made sure the cabin door was shut when they walked outside. "It seems funny being on the bottom of the

Grand Canyon," Josh said. "This morning, we were on the top!"

Ten yards away, the creek flowed past a small beach. A bunch of orange rubber rafts were resting on the sand. A narrow bridge next to the beach let people cross to the cabins on the other side.

Dink dipped his fingers into the creek. "Pretty cold," he said. He noticed something floating and grabbed a small square of wet purple cardboard. He put the trash in his pocket.

The kids saw more cabins like theirs. The dining lodge was larger and stood a few hundred yards from the cabins.

Suddenly a loud noise cut through the dry air.

"What's that?" Dink asked. "It sounds like someone is crying!"

They heard the sound again.

Ruth Rose leaned close to Josh. "The phantom is calling you," she whispered.

CHAPTER 10

"It's the mules!" Josh said. "Let's go see them!"

They ran across the bridge, passed the shower house, and came to the mule barn. About a dozen mules were standing inside the corral.

"There's Poppy!" Ruth Rose said.

"And Rambler," Dink said.

"Sleepy is probably in the barn, sleeping," Josh commented.

"No, there he is, drinking water!" Ruth Rose said.

"Hey, Sleepy, come on over!" Josh

called. He pulled a granola bar from his pocket and tapped it against a post.

All the mules trotted toward him. Josh fed them pieces of the bar while Dink and Ruth Rose scratched behind their ears.

A man in a brown uniform came out of the barn, lugging a bale of hay. He dumped it on the ground and used snippers to cut the wire around the bale. The mules trotted over and began chomping on the hay.

"Howdy," the man said. "Looks like Sleepy, Rambler, and Poppy remember you folks."

"We rode them down here today!" Ruth Rose said.

The man chuckled. "I know you did," he said. "I'm Ron, and I take care of these critters."

"Can we bring them a treat after supper?" Ruth Rose asked.

"They'll be sleeping by then," Ron said. "But come back with a carrot or apple tomorrow morning."

Dink, Josh, and Ruth Rose watched the mules munch the hay. When Ron led them inside the barn, the kids headed back toward their cabin.

Near the creek, Dink noticed a small sign on a post. "The cabins on both sides of Bright Angel Creek were built by architect Mary Colter in 1922," he read.

"Wow, that was almost a hundred years ago!" Josh said.

A man wearing shorts and a baseball cap stepped out of one of the cabins. He walked to a rope that had been strung between two trees. He draped a wet T-shirt over the rope, then went back inside the cabin.

On the beach, a woman was tugging the orange rubber rafts farther up on the sand, away from the creek. A name tag on her brown shirt said BRENDA. The words PHANTOM RANCH were stitched onto a patch on one sleeve.

Brenda was tall, and Dink could see the muscles in her arms as she wrestled with the rafts. Her blond hair was long, and she wore it in a braid.

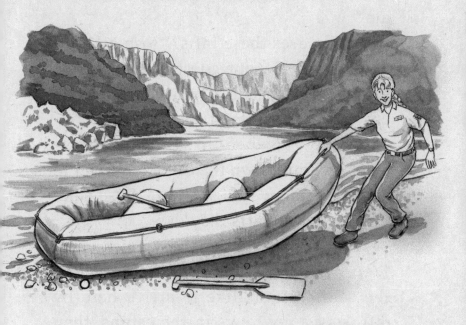

She stood up when she saw the kids. "Hi there," she said, flipping her braid back over her shoulder. "Cabins one and two, right?"

"Yes," Dink said. "We just got here with my uncle a little while ago. I'm Dink Duncan, and my friends are Josh and Ruth Rose."

"We rode here on mules!" Josh said.

"Yes, I know," Brenda said. "Ron told me."

"Who uses these rafts?" Josh asked.

"They're for our guests," she said. "If you're with an adult, you can take one out into the creek and paddle around."

"In my guidebook, it says some people take raft trips down the Colorado River to get to Phantom Ranch," Ruth Rose said. "Are these the rafts they use?"

Brenda wiped her hands on her jeans. "Yep. The river splits off into this creek," she said. "Guests like to arrive here by raft, stay a few days in the cabins, then continue down the river. I pick up the rafts in my truck and bring them back here."

She nodded at the kids, then crossed

the bridge and headed toward the other cabins.

"We should ask your uncle to take us out in one of these rafts!" Josh said.

"Great idea! I wonder if we can get some fishing poles," Dink said. The kids walked toward their own cabin.

As they passed the rafts, Dink saw something purple wedged under a seat. He reached in and pulled out a small square of cardboard.

"What'd you find?" Josh asked.

Dink showed them what looked like a flattened box. It was the size a toy car would fit into.

"This is the second one," Dink said. He reached into his pocket and pulled out the wet cardboard he'd picked up earlier.

"They're the same," he told Josh and Ruth Rose, showing them. "Both are little purple boxes that someone squashed."

"Somebody who likes to litter," Ruth Rose said.

Dink carried the flattened boxes with him as they walked back to their cabin.

When they opened the door, Tommy was sitting on top of the refrigerator. He flapped his wings and squawked, "Tommy is hungry!"

Ruth Rose opened the refrigerator. She found grapes, milk, and a covered plate of chocolate chip cookies.

"Yay, food!" Josh said. "And a note." He plucked a postcard off the refrigerator shelf. On the front was a picture of one of the cabins. PHANTOM RANCH was written over the cabin roof. On the other side, it said: *Welcome to Phantom Ranch, Duncan family. Enjoy the snacks!*

Dink and Josh carried the grapes, cookies, and milk to the table.

"Wait, I have an idea," Ruth Rose said. "Let's sit in front of the window so we can look at the creek while we eat."

Dink and Ruth Rose carried the table and chairs to the window, and Josh went to get Tommy. With the parrot on his shoulder, he walked back across the rug. His toe caught on something, making him stumble.

Josh looked down. "Guys, there's something under this rug," he said. He slid a foot over the spot, then grinned. "Maybe it's a hunk of gold!"

He pulled the rug aside. "Uh-oh," Josh said.

The rug covered a trapdoor.

CHAPTER 11

One edge of the door was raised almost an inch. "That's what I tripped on," Josh said.

"Maybe there's a secret room!" Ruth Rose said.

The kids pried open the door with their fingers. They laid it flat on the floor and peered into a dark space. Three feet below the floor, they saw dirt. A damp smell came up through the opening.

"It's just an empty space under the floor," Dink said.

"My grandfather told me when he was a kid, his house had a space like this,"

Josh said. "They didn't have a fridge, so they kept milk and vegetables there because it was cool."

Dink found a flashlight in a drawer. He jumped into the space, crouched, and shone the beam around.

"What's down there?" Ruth Rose asked.

"Not much," Dink said, wiping a cobweb from his hair. "Some old furniture and spiders."

"They'd better not come up here!" Josh said.

"I'll protect you," Dink said. He got on his knees and crawled a few feet farther, shining the flashlight.

In the center of the space, Dink saw a column of bricks that rose to the wood floor above his head. He sat back and wondered what it was for. Then he remembered the fireplace in the living room. These bricks were the base of the fireplace.

Dink crawled past thick logs that supported the underside of the cabin floor. At the back of the space, sunlight was coming in through a small screened window.

Three broken chairs lay on the dirt near the trapdoor. One of the chairs was missing its seat. In its place was a wide spiderweb. A fat black spider sat in the web. "Stop staring at me," Dink said to the spider.

Then he smiled, thinking about what Josh would do if he were down here. He saw nothing else, so he pulled himself back into the cabin. He used a paper towel to wipe cobwebs off his face. "I didn't see the phantom," he said. "No gold, either." The kids shut the trapdoor and pulled the rug back over it.

"Can we eat now?" Josh asked. "Those cookies are talking to me!"

They found glasses and paper napkins and brought them to the table. The napkins were printed with PHANTOM RANCH in blue letters.

While they snacked on cookies and milk, Josh fed grapes to Tommy. Dink opened the window a few inches so they could hear the creek rushing by.

Suddenly Tommy flew off the chair where he'd been perched and beat his wings against the window. He pecked at

the glass with his beak and squawked, "Roger! Roger!"

Dink looked out the window. He didn't see anyone. "Nobody is there, Tommy," he told the parrot. "No Roger."

Tommy attacked the glass again with his feet and wings, calling out, "Roger!"

Ruth Rose got up. "I'll go take a look," she said, and opened the door. Josh held Tommy against his chest until the parrot settled down.

Through the window, Dink watched Ruth Rose walk to the creek. She crossed the bridge to the two cabins on the other side. Then she turned around and hurried back.

"I think I know why Tommy is upset!" Ruth Rose said, rushing past them into the bedroom.

She came back with her binoculars and sat at the table. "Remember the T-shirt that man hung on the line?" she asked. "Parker Stone wears one just like it on TV. And he was wearing it yesterday in the hot-air balloon. Tommy must have recognized the shirt!"

"But isn't it just any old T-shirt?" Josh asked.

"No," Ruth Rose said. "It has that circle with *RTTR* written inside."

"I remember," Dink said. "The letters stand for *Roger to the Rescue.*"

Ruth Rose pointed out the window. "You can see the shirt from here," she said. "Tommy must think Parker is over there!"

Josh grabbed the binoculars. "You're right, Roger Good wears that T-shirt on every show," he said.

"So do a lot of other people," Dink said. "You can buy those shirts on his website."

"But it *could* be Parker's shirt," Ruth Rose said.

Dink looked at her. "What would his T-shirt be doing here?" he asked.

Ruth Rose started pacing around the room. "He got taken near the Grand Canyon," she said. "Maybe the kidnappers brought him down here!"

"Here?" Josh asked.

Ruth Rose nodded. "Phantom Ranch would be a perfect place for the kidnappers to hide Parker till they got the three million dollars!" she said.

CHAPTER 12

The kids stared out the window. On the rope line, the T-shirt moved in the breeze.

"If that *is* Parker's T-shirt," Ruth Rose went on, "he might be in that cabin! And the man who hung up the shirt could be one of the kidnappers!"

"Let's go knock on the door," Josh suggested.

"Guys, tons of people buy those T-shirts from the website," Dink said. "That one probably belongs to the guy staying in that cabin."

"Okay, you could be right," Ruth Rose said. "But can we just walk by the cabin?

Maybe we'll see something through the windows."

"Like what?" Dink asked.

"Like Parker Stone watching TV and eating a burger!" Josh said.

Dink laughed. "All right, I guess it wouldn't hurt to take a look," he said. "But let's leave Tommy here. We don't need him getting all upset again."

Josh put Tommy in the cat carrier and gave him a grape. The kids walked across the bridge and up the path toward the cabins. The clothesline holding the T-shirt was next to cabin four. Up close, it was easy to see *RTTR* inside a circle.

"That's exactly like the one Parker was wearing yesterday," Ruth Rose whispered. "Can you see anything through the window?"

"Nope," Josh said.

The cabin door opened, and a woman appeared. "Can I help you kids?" she asked.

She was wearing a sweatshirt and shorts. Her blond hair was draped over one shoulder, and she twirled the ends with her fingers.

Dink stared at the woman. *Where have I seen her before?* he wondered.

"Um, we thought we saw something moving over here," Ruth Rose said.

"Moving?" the woman said.

"Someone told us there are bears in the Grand Canyon!" Josh said. "We thought we'd check it out."

Dink tried not to giggle. *Josh checking out a bear?*

"Well, I hope you're wrong!" the woman said. "Let me ask my husband."

She turned around and called into the cabin, "Flip, have you seen any bears around here?"

The man who had hung the T-shirt on the clothesline came to the door. He was skinny and had a pointy beard. "There better not be any," he said. "You guys staying here?"

"Right over there," Dink said, pointing across the creek. "I'm Dink, and my friends are Josh and Ruth Rose."

"Nice to meet you," the man said. "I'm Flip, and this is my wife, Heidi."

Dink glanced through the open cabin door. He saw a table and chairs in front of a fireplace, the same as in their own cabin. The floor was bare, and the rug was rolled up, off to one side. Through the bedroom doorway, Dink could see a neatly made bed. He didn't see any sign of Parker Stone.

"Well, see you later," Flip said. He and Heidi went inside and closed the door.

The kids walked back across the bridge to their cabin. They sat at the table and looked out the window. "Well," Josh said, "Dink is right. The T-shirt must belong to that guy or his wife. Parker must not be there, unless he's tied up in the bathroom."

Dink took a sip of his milk and picked up his cookie. The cookie never made it to his mouth because his hand froze in mid-air. "Guys, I was wrong," he whispered.

"About what?" Ruth Rose asked.

"About Parker Stone," Dink said. "I think he *is* here at Phantom Ranch!"

CHAPTER 13

Josh and Ruth Rose looked at Dink. He was holding his cookie in one hand and his milk glass in the other.

"What made you change your mind?" Ruth Rose asked.

Dink dipped his chin toward the table. "Read what it says on my napkin," he said.

"It says *Phantom Ranch,* the same as ours," Josh said.

Dink set his cookie on the napkin, covering the first four letters in PHANTOM. He placed his milk glass over the CH in RANCH. "Now what does it say?" he asked.

Ruth Rose and Josh looked at the letters not covered by Dink's cookie and milk glass. The only letters they could see now were TOM RAN.

Ruth Rose's mouth fell open.

Josh nearly choked. "That's what Parker wrote in the dirt!" he cried.

Dink nodded. "What if the kidnappers mentioned Phantom Ranch when they were talking to each other, and Parker heard them?" he asked. "Then he wrote that on the ground with his foot, like Josh said!"

"And someone's feet messed up the rest of the letters!" Ruth Rose said.

"That woman looked familiar," Dink said. "Flip's wife, Heidi. I think I've seen her someplace before."

The kids stared out the window at cabin four. The T-shirt flapped in the breeze.

"I have a feeling Parker *is* inside that cabin," Dink said. "They have a rug like ours, but it's rolled up. I'll bet there's a space under the floor, too. Like in this cabin."

"Parker could be under the floor!" Josh said. "They keep the rug rolled up so they can open the trapdoor to feed him!"

Dink nodded. "That's what I'm thinking," he said. "And another thing. Remember those two purple cardboards I found? I think they were *raisin boxes*. Parker feeds Tommy raisins on his TV show, and raisins come in little purple boxes!"

"On the show, Roger keeps raisins in his pockets," Ruth Rose said. "The boxes must have fallen out when the kidnappers were bringing him here!"

"Or Parker dropped the boxes on purpose, hoping someone would find them," Dink said.

Just then, someone knocked on the cabin door. Tommy squawked, and the kids jumped.

The door opened, and Dink's uncle walked in. "You guys look like you've seen a ghost," Uncle Warren said. "What's up?"

"You scared us," Dink said. "We were just . . . having a snack."

His uncle glanced at the plate of cookies on the table. "Dinner's in about an hour, guys. Will you still be hungry?"

"I will!" Josh said.

"Tommy is hungry!" the parrot yelled. "Tommy wants raisins!"

Uncle Warren laughed. "Okay. I'm going to find a shady tree and read for a while," he said. "You guys want to grab a book and join me?"

"Um, sorry," Dink said. "We have to stay here. We're doing a . . . a . . ."

"A project," Ruth Rose said.

"Yeah, a secret project," Dink added.

"Good. Then I'll leave you to it," Uncle Warren said, heading for the door.

"Why didn't you tell him?" Ruth Rose asked when the door closed.

"Because he wouldn't like what I'm going to do tonight," Dink said.

Josh's eyes got huge. "What're you going to do?" he asked.

Dink grinned. "What would Roger do?" he asked.

"He'd figure out how to get inside that cabin!" Ruth Rose whispered.

Dink nodded. "Exactly," he said.

"But how?" Josh asked. "Those people are there!"

"Come outside. I want to show you something," Dink said. He led Josh and Ruth Rose to the back of their cabin. Partly hidden by weeds was a small opening covered with a wire screen.

"Remember when I went down in the crawl space?" Dink said. "I saw light, and it was coming through this screen."

"But this is *our* cabin, Dink," Josh said. "Parker is in *their* cabin."

"That architect built these cabins at the same time," Dink said. "They all look alike, so the other cabin probably has an opening like this one."

"Leading to a secret room underneath!" Ruth Rose said. "Wait a second."

She ran the twenty yards to Dink's uncle's cabin. A minute later, she was back. "Your uncle's cabin has an opening just like this one," she said.

"That's what I thought," Dink said. "They probably all do." He poked at the screen with his foot. "This will come out easy. I think I can squeeze through the opening in Flip and Heidi's cabin."

"When?" Josh asked.

"Tonight while everyone is at supper," Dink said. "It'll only take a minute to find out if I'm right."

"Are you crazy?" Josh said. "If Flip and Heidi *are* the kidnappers and they catch you, you'll disappear, too!"

"But what if I'm right and Parker Stone *is* under their cabin?" Dink asked. "We have to try!"

"That's what Roger Good would do," Ruth Rose said. "And we're going to help, right, Josh?"

Josh closed his eyes. Then he opened them and grinned. "Dink, Josh, and Ruth Rose to the rescue!"

Dink told them the rest of his plan.

CHAPTER 14

It was dark when the kids and Uncle Warren walked to the dining room. There were about twenty people inside. Some were sitting at tables, eating. Others were in line, holding trays.

A long table held platters of fried chicken, roasted potatoes, green beans, a salad, and lots more. Dessert was brownies. Drink choices were milk, juice boxes, or iced tea. The kids each took a small piece of chicken, a few potatoes, and a juice box.

"Did you eat too many cookies?" Uncle Warren asked when they brought their small servings to the table. His tray held mounds of chicken, potatoes, and salad.

Dink grinned at his uncle. "Sorry," he said. "I guess we're not that hungry."

Everyone began to eat. Dink looked around and saw Luke and Junior sitting with Ron. Dink waved, and Luke winked at him.

All three kids were looking for Flip and Heidi, but the couple wasn't in the room.

Dink raised his eyebrows at Josh and Ruth Rose. If Flip and Heidi didn't leave their cabin, the plan wouldn't work!

After about ten minutes, Dink kicked Josh and Ruth Rose under the table. They all put down their forks. Josh rubbed his stomach and said, "Gosh, I'm full! I don't even have room for dessert!"

"Me too," Ruth Rose said. She placed her napkin on the table.

"I can't eat any more," Dink said.

"Can we please be excused?"

Uncle Warren gazed at the kids. "Well, this is a first," he said. "As you can see, I have barely started on my dinner. Go on back, and I'll catch up with you later."

The kids raced to their cabin, keeping an eye out for Flip and Heidi on the path. Back in the cabin, they rushed to the window. Ruth Rose trained her binoculars on the cabins across the creek. Tommy was in the bedroom, asleep in the cat carrier.

"Are they in their cabin?" Dink asked.

"I don't see them," Ruth Rose said.

Two women came out of cabin three. They wore boots, hiking shorts, and fleece jackets. They followed the path toward the dining lodge.

The kids kept their eyes on cabin four. Lights went on behind the curtains, but nobody came through the door.

It was growing darker. Fireflies darted among the bushes. Something black flew

past. Dink thought it was a bat.

"Maybe they ate a lot of cookies, too," Josh said. "Maybe they're not going to eat supper. Or they got takeout!"

Ruth Rose giggled. "No one's going to bring take-out food nine miles down the canyon trail," she said.

Dink's stomach was doing flip-flops. He tore one of the napkins into tiny pieces. He was sweating under his shirt.

"Look!" Ruth Rose said.

A lantern over the door to cabin four blinked on, lighting up the small porch. The door opened, and Flip and Heidi stepped outside. They held hands as they followed the path to the dining room.

"Okay," Dink said, letting out his breath. "Plan Parker now begins!"

"Be careful, dude," Josh said. He left and hurried across the bridge. Josh's part of the plan was spying on the dining room. If Flip and Heidi came out, Josh would race back to warn Dink.

"I hope you find Parker," Ruth Rose said to Dink. Then she left. Her job was to stand on the bridge, pretending to be catching fireflies. When she blew her whistle, it meant *Get out fast!*

Dink was the last to leave the cabin. He wore a black T-shirt and dark jeans. He pulled on a baseball cap to cover his light hair. Ruth Rose's Swiss Army knife was in his pocket, and he carried her flashlight.

He crossed the bridge, pretending not to see Ruth Rose standing a few feet away from him. "Good luck!" she whispered.

Dink hurried to cabin four. The porch lantern lit the front yard. He walked around to the back, where it was totally dark. He switched on the flashlight but kept a hand over the beam. A small amount of light shone through his fingers.

Behind some weeds, Dink found the wire screen low on the cabin's rear wall.

Kneeling, he quickly pulled the weeds away. The opening was about two feet wide, like the one on his cabin.

The screen was set inside a wood frame. Using the big blade on Ruth Rose's knife, Dink sliced through the screen. He peeled the wire away from the frame and set it on the ground. The opening was wide enough for him to crawl through.

Dink shone the flashlight into the dark space. He saw only dirt and the supports that held the floor up. He felt his heart thumping in his chest. His hand holding the flashlight shook. He whispered, "Parker?" and heard no answer.

Dink swallowed, but his throat was dry. He held the flashlight in his mouth as he put his head and arms through the opening. His shoulders scraped against the wood frame.

Dink's hands found the dirt floor, and he pulled himself all the way in. He knew he couldn't stand, so he crawled forward.

The flashlight's beam jiggled as he held it in his teeth.

The dirt felt damp under Dink's hands and knees. A spiderweb caught on his left ear, and he swatted it away. The large supporting logs reminded him of dinosaur legs. A broken bed frame lying on the dirt looked like a skeleton.

Dink crawled toward the center of the cabin. He saw a brick column like the one under his cabin floor. He knew it was under the fireplace, near the trapdoor.

Kneeling next to the bricks, Dink aimed the flashlight toward where he thought the trapdoor should be.

The light fell on Parker Stone's face.

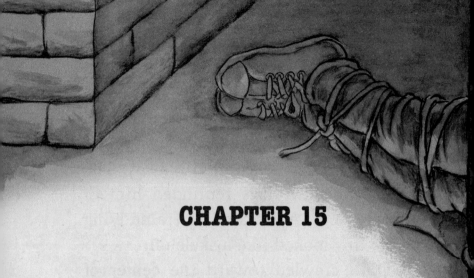

CHAPTER 15

Parker was lying on a blanket. Gray tape covered his mouth. A bandana was tied over his eyes. His hands and legs were tied with clothesline rope, which was wrapped around one of the floor supports.

Dink hurried forward on his hands and knees. "Parker, can you hear me?" he whispered.

Parker grunted and wiggled his feet.

"Awesome!" Dink said. "I'm Dink. My friends and I are going to rescue you!"

Parker grunted again and tried to lift his shoulders.

Dink removed the bandana from

Parker's head and pulled the tape off his mouth. His face was smudged with dirt and leftover food.

"Dude, am I glad to see you!" Parker said. His voice sounded croaky, as if he hadn't used it in a while. "Where are those jerks who stuck me down here?"

"Flip and Heidi are eating supper," Dink said. "We have to hurry!"

Parker sat up and struggled.

"There are three of them," Parker said. "There's another woman, in a brown uniform. She brought us here in a rubber raft! I think Heidi is her sister."

Dink thought about all the women they had met at Phantom Ranch. Heidi had long blond hair. And so did Brenda. "Maybe it's Brenda," Dink said. "She takes care of the rafts on the beach."

"Can you untie these knots?" Parker asked. He struggled against the ropes.

"I brought a knife," Dink said. "Hold still." The blade was sharp, and soon

Parker's hands and legs were loose. "Don't try to stand up. You'll hit your head!"

"How do we get out of here?" Parker whispered. "How'd you get in?"

"There's a small opening," Dink whispered. "It's over—"

Suddenly Dink heard a whistle. He put his hand on Parker's arm. Then he heard a second whistle.

"That's my friend's signal!" Dink said. "Someone's coming!" He grabbed the flashlight and crawled away as fast as he could. He felt Parker behind him.

Then he heard Josh's voice coming through the opening. "Dude, they're coming! They're almost at the cabin!"

Dink froze and turned off the flashlight. Parker's head bumped against him.

"They usually bring me food," Parker whispered. "They'll open the trapdoor! When they don't see—"

Just then, they heard heavy footsteps thudding over their heads. Then they heard a creaking sound as the trapdoor was lifted. A square of light fell onto the dirt floor.

Flip yelled, "He's gone! The ropes are cut!"

Flip's head and shoulders appeared upside down through the trapdoor opening.

The crawl space was dark, so Dink didn't think Flip could see them. But he grabbed Parker's arm, and they both slipped behind the brick column. Dink held his breath.

"Heidi, where's that flashlight?" Flip yelled. His head and shoulders disappeared inside the cabin.

"Let's go!" Dink said.

The two boys scuttled across the damp dirt. Dink shoved his head through the opening, and Josh and Ruth Rose pulled him through the frame.

"Did you find Parker?" Ruth Rose asked.

Parker's face appeared. "He sure did!" he said.

Dink, Josh, and Ruth Rose grabbed Parker's hands to tug him through the opening. His head and arms made it, but then he stopped. "My shoulders won't fit!" he said.

"But I got through!" Dink said.

"I'm bigger than you!" Parker said.

Parker pulled himself back inside the dark space. He lay on his back and braced his boots against the wood frame. Then he began kicking the frame as hard as he could. The wood was a hundred years old and shattered easily. A minute later, the four kids were racing away from the cabin.

They stopped and caught their breath behind the mule barn. "Where are we going?" Parker asked. "Do you guys know your way around here?"

"We need to get help!" Dink said.

"Let's go find your uncle," Ruth Rose said to Dink.

"Maybe he's still eating," Josh said. "Follow me!"

They raced through the dark until they saw the lights of the dining room. People were walking out, chatting with each other.

Dink saw Uncle Warren standing with Ron, Luke, and Junior. The kids ran up to the men. "This is Parker Stone!" Dink told his uncle. "He was tied up in one of the cabins! His kidnappers are still there!"

"Which cabin?" his uncle asked.

"Number four!" Ruth Rose said. "Across the creek from ours!"

They all ran, with Ron taking the lead. Dink heard his uncle filling in the other men about Parker Stone's kidnapping. When they reached cabin four, the door was wide open. Light spilled onto the porch.

"They're not here!" Luke said.

"Yes, they are!" Ruth Rose said. "Look!"

She pointed to the little beach. Three people were dragging one of the rubber rafts into the water.

Ron, Luke, and Junior bolted toward

the creek. They surrounded Flip, Heidi, and Brenda. When the kidnappers realized there was no way out, they put their hands up in surrender.

Parker walked over and looked at his kidnappers. "Busted," he said.

CHAPTER 16

Ron, Luke, and Junior led the kidnappers toward the ranger station. A police helicopter would take them to the sheriff's office.

The three kids and Uncle Warren waited while Parker called his parents on the landline. Then they all crossed the bridge and walked to cabin two. Parker used the kids' bathroom to wash his face and hands.

They shared the rest of the milk and cookies while Parker told the kids and Dink's uncle what had happened at Blue Meadow. Tommy sat on his shoulder.

"We were in the woods when two guys jumped us," Parker told them. "They put a pillowcase over Max's head. I kicked one of the guys really hard in the knee. I'd have kicked him again, but they both jumped on me and tied me to a tree. They had a truck there, and they ran over to it and pulled out a big rug."

"Did you write *Phantom Ranch* in the dirt?" Ruth Rose asked.

Parker grinned. "Yeah. When they were tying me to the tree, I saw a yellow-and-brown Phantom Ranch patch on one guy's shirt," he said. "Actually, I realize now that it was a woman, not a guy. Anyway, I saw the same yellow-and-brown logo on the truck's bumper sticker. So when they weren't looking, I tried to write *Phantom Ranch* with my boot. I could only write *Phantom Ran* before they came to untie me."

"That is so cool!" Josh said. "Just like Roger Good!"

"A brilliant move, young man!" Uncle Warren said.

"We found what you wrote!" Ruth Rose said. "But their feet must have erased the first four letters in *Phantom*."

"They rolled me up inside the rug and put it in the back of the truck," Parker continued. "The guys drove like crazy, and it was real bumpy. Then they stopped and dragged the rug and me onto the ground. They took the rug off and held a smelly cloth over my nose and mouth. It put me to sleep, and when I came to, I was where you found me—tied up in the dark."

"We found your raisin boxes, too," Dink said.

Parker nodded. "I figured my kidnapping would be on TV," he said. "A lot of people know I feed Tommy raisins on the show, so I hoped someone would find the boxes and figure out I dropped them."

"Is that your shirt on the clothesline?" Josh asked.

"Yup," Parker said. "When Flip and Heidi brought me a hamburger, I ate all the mustard and made myself throw up. It smelled gross! I hoped they'd wash my shirt and hang it outside. I thought someone would recognize it from the show."

"Tommy did!" Dink said. "He saw your shirt through our window and got excited. You should have seen him trying to get to it!"

Parker patted Tommy's head. "My buddy Tommy has excellent vision," he said. "Good old parrot!"

"So Flip, Heidi, and Brenda planned the whole thing," Uncle Warren said. "They asked your parents for ransom."

"They did?" Parker asked. "How much?"

"Three million dollars," Dink's uncle told him.

Parker sipped his milk and stared out the window. "I think there's someone else," he said. "When they were rolling me in the rug, I heard one of them ask about the money. Flip said, '*The boss* will bring our share in a couple of days.' "

"So who's this *boss*?" Josh asked.

Dink watched Parker stare out the window. He had tears in his eyes. "I think the boss is Max," he said. "My agent."

"Mr. Kurve?" Dink asked.

Parker nodded. "A couple of weeks ago, Max got a new insurance policy for me. If I got hurt real bad, he told me, the policy would pay three million dollars. Or if I got kidnapped."

Parker looked sad. "It was *Max's* idea to come to the Grand Canyon and go for a balloon ride. *He* made me walk with him into those woods. *He* knew about the insurance policy."

"But what about the blood on his face and shirt?" Josh asked.

"What blood?" Parker asked.

Dink told Parker about Maxwell Kurve running out of the woods with his shirt and face all bloody.

"I thought there was something funny about that blood," Dink said. "Mr. Kurve told us the kidnappers put the pillow-case over his head, then punched him. If they'd done that, the pillowcase would have been bloody."

"But it wasn't," Ruth Rose said. "The pillowcase was clean."

Dink nodded. "Even if they'd put the pillowcase on *after* they slugged him, there would still have been blood on it," he said.

"I'll bet a million bucks they didn't really hit Max," Parker said. "He and I used to practice karate together. He knows how to fake getting punched."

"So that means there was no blood, right?" Josh said.

"Oh my gosh!" Ruth Rose cried. She ran into the bedroom and came back with the nail polish bottle. She twisted off the cap and handed the bottle to Parker. "Smell it," she told him.

Parker took a sniff. "It's stage blood,"
he said. "They use it in movies and on
TV. You mix red food coloring, sugar, and
cocoa in a blender. Where'd you find it?"

"In the woods," Dink said. "Near where they grabbed you."

"Max must've squirted this stuff on his face and shirt *after* he took the pillow-case off," Parker said.

"Then he threw the bottle in the stream," Dink said.

Parker wiped his eyes. "Max planned it all," he said. "I thought he was my friend, but all he wanted was money."

The kids sat and watched Tommy clean his wing feathers with his beak.

"What are you going to do about Mr. Kurve?" Dink asked Parker. "He doesn't know you escaped from Heidi and Flip."

"My dad told me to call him and my mom after they had a chance to talk to our lawyer," Parker said. "I'll tell them about Max, and they'll arrest him."

"Do you want us to come with you to call your parents?" Ruth Rose asked.

"That would be great," Parker said.

"Cool!" Josh said. "Can Tommy ride on me?"

Parker transferred Tommy to Josh's shoulder, and they walked toward the ranger station.

Parker had a long talk with his mother and father. He explained why he thought Maxwell Kurve had planned the kidnapping. Two hours later, Maxwell was arrested.

Parker's parents told him that they planned to fly to Arizona the next morning. For tonight, Parker would stay with his new friends, Dink, Josh, and Ruth Rose, in their cabin.

In cabin two, the four kids were playing Scrabble.

"My mom wants to give you guys a reward," Parker said. "And I have an amazingly awesome idea!"

"We don't need a reward," Dink said.

"Except maybe your autograph," Ruth Rose added.

"What's your amazingly awesome idea?" Josh asked Parker.

"How about you guys come on my next show?" Parker asked.

"Really?" all three kids said.

"Cool!" Josh said. "Can we call the show *Josh to the Rescue*?"

Parker shook his head. "No way, Ray."